Nessie the Mannerless Monster

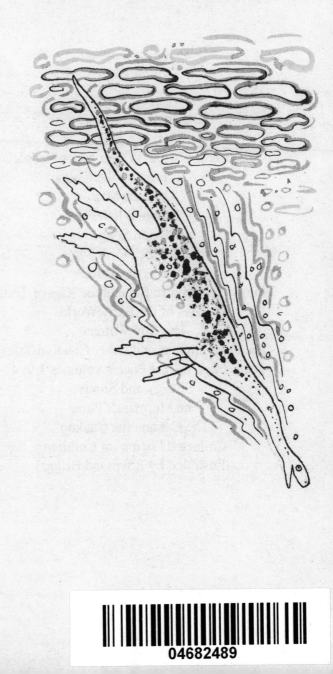

by the same author
for children

How the Whale Became
Meet My Folks!
The Earth-Owl and Other Moon People
The Coming of the Kings
The Iron Man
Moon-Whales
Season Songs
Under the North Star
What is the Truth?
Ffangs the Vampire Bat and the Kiss of Truth
Tales of the Early World
The Iron Woman
The Dreamfighter and Other Creation Tales
Collected Animal Poems volumes 1 to 4
Shaggy and Spotty
The Mermaid's Purse
The Cat and the Cuckoo
Collected Poems for Children
(illustrated by Raymond Briggs)

Nessie the Mannerless Monster

Ted Hughes

illustrated by Gerald Rose

faber and faber

First published in 1964
by Faber and Faber Limited
Bloomsbury House
74–7 Great Russell Street
London WC1B 3DA
This paperback edition first published in 2011

Photoset by Parker Typesetting Service, Leicester
Printed in England by CPI Bookmarque, Croydon, UK

A CIP record for this book
is available from the British Library

ISBN 978–0–571–27449–9

2 4 6 8 10 9 7 5 3 1

Nessie the Mannerless Monster

In Scotland is a Loch.
At the bottom of this Loch, in the
    pitch black,
A monster lives, called Nessie. It is just
    her luck.
She is about the size of a truck,
But shaped like an old sock,
With a long worm of a neck.
She is beginning to feel sick.

She is sick with sorrow. 'Nobody thinks
    I exist.
They all say my time has passed.
They say I am a fairy beast.
I do not want to boast,
But I will make myself known or bust.'
So Nessie rises in a great burst
Of spray, she smashes the water to mist,
She scuds around doing her worst.

But people just keep on driving past.
They say: 'No, No! Such things do not
exist.'
Soon she grows tired and has to lie there,
having a rest.

Then in a rage, she outs on to the road.
She says: 'I don't want to be rude,
But after all, I have my pride.'
She says: 'I am going to make a raid
On Edinburgh.' Then all the tourists
    cried
'What's that? What's that? Oh, Oh, let me
    hide!'
And they crashed their cars into the
    roadside.
They covered their eyes hoping the sight
    would fade.
But Nessie walked straight on, she paid no
    heed.

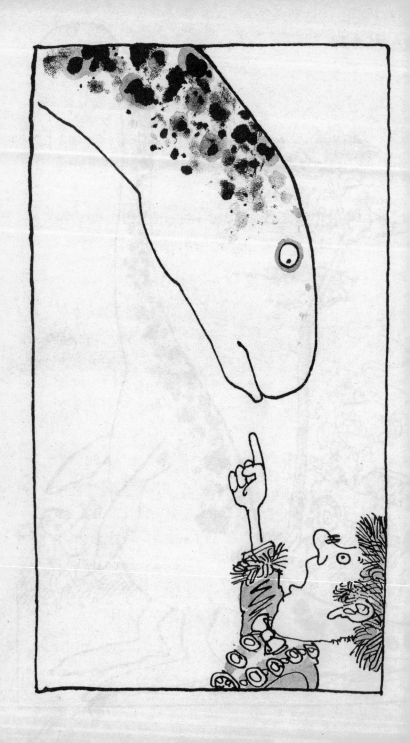

The Mayor of Edinburgh nearly had a fit
When he saw Nessie. 'Look at it! Look at
   it!'
He cried, and fainted right there on the
   spot.

But the police said, 'Whose is that huge
   cat?
It is blocking our traffic more than a bit.
Divert it south to London.' So that was
   that.
Nessie had not opened her mouth and she
   was out,
Tramping south towards London alone
   and on foot.

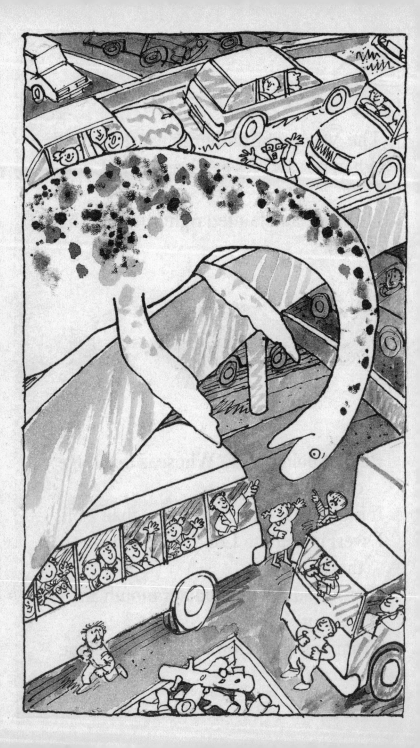

As she was tramping down through
   Northumberland
Up out of a ditch pops this fox-hound.
'Look!' he howls, 'A fox as long as a brass
   band!'
The other hounds come running up and
   all stare stunned.
Then Wow-wow-wow! they chase Nessie
   over the ploughed land,
And into a wood and out at the far end,
Then into a meadow and round with the
   cows and round.

'I'm no fox,' cries Nessie, but they can't
    understand.
She dives into and just fills up a
    duckpond.
The huntsmen gallop up. When they see
    Nessie making a stand
They turn away their horses and tuck their
    hounds under
Their arms and creep off home quaking
    with fear and no wonder,
Seeing Nessie there in the duckpond like
    a coal-black forty-foot gander.

She marches south into Yorkshire, the
   greatest shire.
'Now,' she says, 'I've heard there are
   honest folk here
Who will all cry "Nessie!" the minute I
   appear.'
But what does she find? The streets are all
   empty and bare.
Everybody sits indoors in front of the TV
   with a dead stare.

There is nothing in the streets but cats,
    dogs and the odd parked car.
She peers in at the windows and whistles
    but nobody can hear
For the TV and its laughter and uproar
    and gunfire.
There is no other sign of life in all
    Yorkshire anywhere,
Till she meets a little boy and he shouts:
    'Hey, you. Get out of here.'

Next, travelling through the woods to
  avoid the cars
She meets Sir Mimms Culdimple
  Bagforkhumberly-parse.
'You'll stay to dine,' offers that gent, with
  a laugh, 'of course?'
And he rips off an utterly dumbfounding
  curse
That kills a big orange horsefly on the ear
  of a nearby horse.

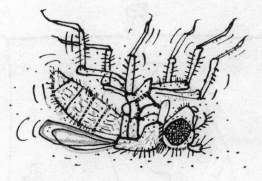

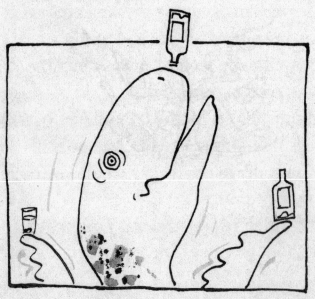

Nessie devours partridges, pheasants,
    pigs' heads, pike and parts of hares.
She drinks whisky and wine until it pours
    out of her ears.

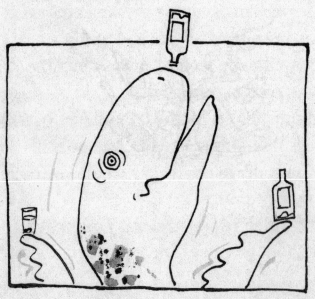

Then she snaps up the servants, the cook
    too in spite of his roars.
She swallows a settee for wadding, the
    whole item disappears,
And finishes off her host in one gulp, and
    says: 'That was a solid first course.'
And falls down on the carpet and without
    apology snores –
All of which proves she was completely
    without manners and a perfect monster.

Next, she came up with ten thousand
   people and then some.
They all marched packed together, with
   here and there a drum.
They carry banners with the words: 'Ban
   The Bomb.'
They are laughing and singing and Nessie
   thinks: 'Is this a party? Can I come?'
'Be our mascot,' they cry, 'O peaceful
   beast, beautiful and dumb.'
So Nessie marches along at the head of
   them.

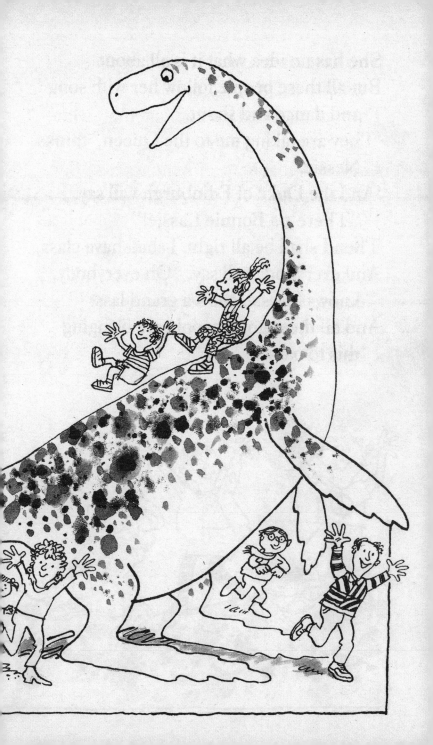

She has no idea what it is all about
But all these people follow her with song
   and dance and shout.
'They are taking me to the Queen,' thinks
   Nessie,
'And the Duke of Edinburgh will say,
   "There's a Bonnie Lassie!"
Then I shall be all right, I shall have class,
And everybody will say, "Oh everybody
   knows Nessie, she's a grand lass."
And all these good people are bringing
   this to pass.'

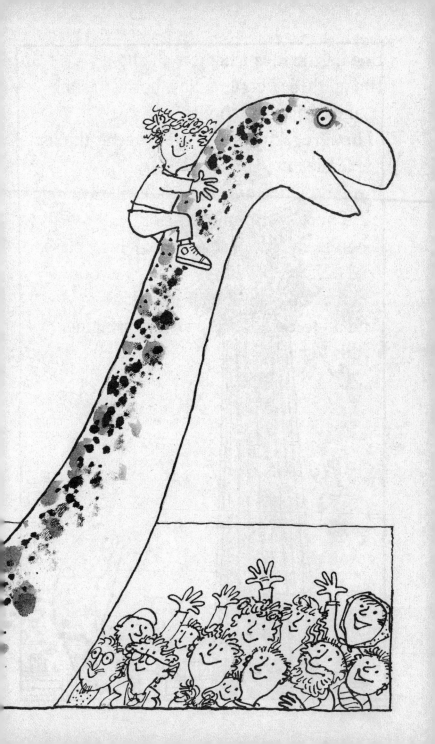

But when they got to the heart of London
and Trafalgar Square
Somehow everybody disappeared into
thin air
Leaving hundreds of policemen yawning
there.
Whenever she asked a policeman the way
to the Queen, he politely directed her to
the zoo.
And so she followed the policeman's
finger, which is what people in London
do.

When Nessie walked through the zoo
  fence
The gorilla burst his bars and fled into the
  far distance.

The keepers jumped clean out of their
  clothes at the first glance
And hid behind the tigers which stood in a
  dumb trance.

The wolves fell into a dead faint at once.
The elephants gave up all thoughts of
  defence.

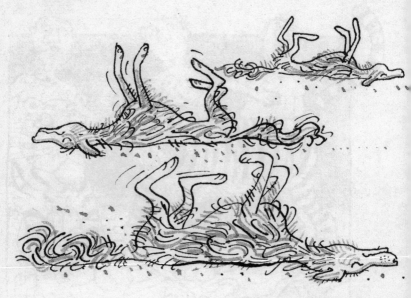

The eagles went rigid and cried: 'We are
  only weathervanes.'
The snakes murmured: 'Take no notice of
  us, we are only vines.'

The tortoises pulled in their heads and legs and whispered: 'We are stones.'

The lions lay still with eyes closed and
    tried to look like sand-dunes.
And Nessie wandered around saying: 'Are
    all these creatures Queens?'

Till up came the small mammal-house
   keeper, braver than the rest.
'We have no place,' he said, 'for your sort
   of beast.
Go to Kensington Museum, that would be
   best.
They have all your cousins there, prettily
   encased.
You can meet them all and have a real
   feast.'

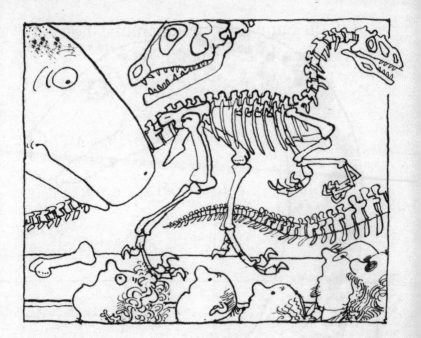

'Thank you, thank you!' cried Nessie, 'I
    will do just as you suggest.
I was beginning to feel weary and
    depressed.
I never knew I had cousins. When they see
    me won't they be surprised.'

In Kensington Museum all the curators
    stared.
They stared at Nessie, they had never
    seen anything so weird.

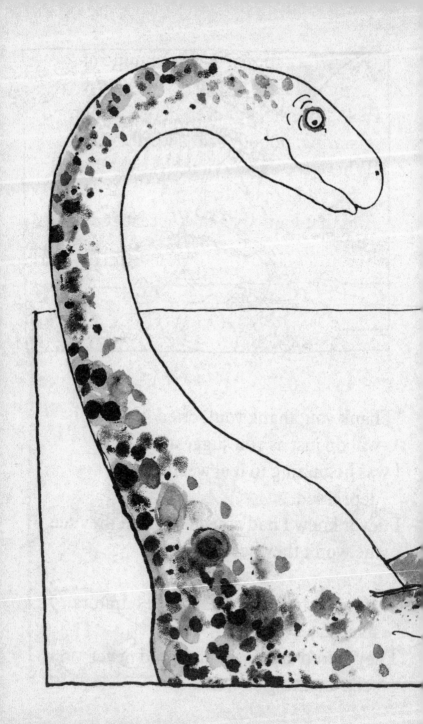

'Where are these cousins of mine of
    whom I have heard?'
Asked Nessie, but everybody went on
    staring, nobody said a word.
'Where are they?' cried Nessie, 'They'll
    tell you I do truly exist,
And that I am not a fairy-beast and not a
    dream-beast.'

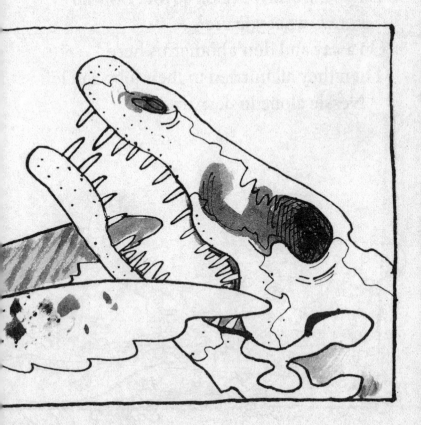

Then up spoke a world-famous scientist:
'Impostor! You are impossible! If you
    were extinct and no more
Indeed I would say you were a Plesiosaur.
We have plenty of the bones of that beast
    which in its day was not at all rare.
But all Plesiosaurs, say our books, have
    been dead a million year.
Yet you are alive. Look at you. So who
    knows what you are?
Go away and don't bother us here.'
Then they all hurried to their jobs and left
    Nessie alone in despair.

Nessie wandered sadly along High Street.
'Get a move on,' snarled all the taxi-
    drivers, leaning out.
A huge lorry bumped her backside with
    hoot after hoot.
Tourists gasped: 'Look, quick, another
    famous London sight.'
Londoners thought she was an advert, for
    a circus coming that night.
Policemen roared: 'Drive on the left, idiot,
    not the right.'
What with all the noise and crowds Nessie
    was in a great fright.

But all at once a voice from the crowd
   roared 'Ness!'
Her eyes popped when she heard her
   name, joy made her nearly delirious.

It was a wretched Scots writer of verses,
    Willis by name, and he was penniless,
But he knew a monster when he saw one,
    Oh yes.
'Nessie!' he cried, and he gave her flipper
    a great kiss.
She told him her woes and he cried: 'Alas!
    Alas! Alas!

We shall go without hesitation to the
  palace.
Let me ride and you run.' And so in no
  time they were off at a great pace.

When they galloped up to Buckingham
    Palace, guards barred the way.
'Dogs on a leash,' they ordered, and, 'No
    visitors today.'
So Willis cried: 'The Queen's greatest
    subject has something to say –
Nessie here is the Queen's greatest
    subject, I will have you know.'
But the guards just bristled their
    moustaches, and it was no go.

Whereupon Nessie simply ran over the
  guards and left them looking for their
  hats:
But then the Palace Army, which always
  waits,
The Palace Army which protects the
  Queen from all dangers and frights,

Did not stand staring like dumb mountain
  goats.
They barked commands, scampered to
  their posts, manned their guns, gloated
  through the gunsights,
And Nessie and Willis were at any
  moment about to be blown to bits.

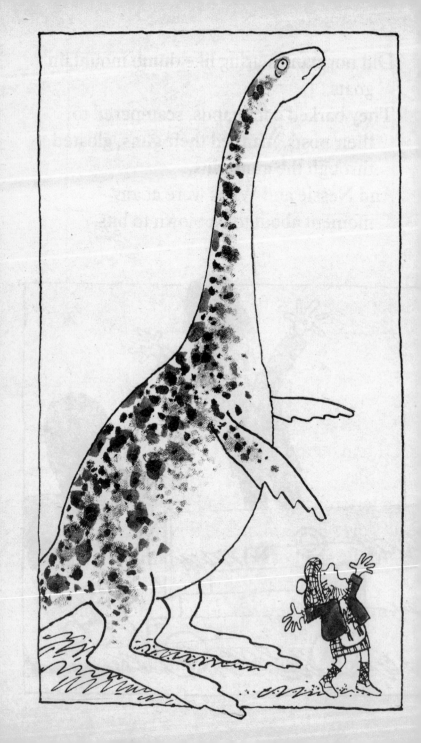

'Stop, stop!' shouted Willis, 'Let's have a
   peace-talk.'
Then out on to her balcony the Queen
   came for a look,
Her crown on her head, her stoatskins
   over her arm, to see this freak.
At the sight of Nessie she uttered a
   strange croak,
But then, like a true Queen, most politely
   she spoke:
Saying: 'What do you want, for heaven's
   sake?'

Then Willis up and gave his speech on
   Nessie's behalf.
In no time at all he told how her times
   were so tough,
In no time at all he told the causes of her
   grief,
Living up there in Scotland, monstrous
   beyond belief.

And the Queen was touched with concern
   for this gigantic national waif.
Then the Duke made a joke, and the
   Queen gave a laugh:
'You shall be Vice-Regent of Scotland,
   Wales and Northern Ireland,' she said,
   'For the rest of your life.'

And so it comes about that Nessie reigns
in Loch Ness.
On Sundays all along the shores the
people press,
The bands of the Coldstream Guards and
Scottish Light Infantry play *en masse*.

Nessie cruises up and down with a
coronet on her head.
She is delighted, she never had it so good.
And Willis is a Civil Servant, he sees that
she's well fed,
And he's delighted too, he gets so well
paid.

And what finer life can there be than
    living on the shores of a marvellous lake
With a pet monster, and doing as you like.
The scientists come in tribes, for a look.
Nessie invents stories about her ancestors
    and they write them all down in their
    book.
And whenever the Queen visits Scotland,
    she visits this Loch,
Then she and Nessie sit sipping tea and
    have a really good talk.

having a tea party